The Lost Children

Kevin D.N. Lawson

The Lost Children. Kevin D.N. Lawson. Copyright © September 22, 2012. All Rights Reserved.

Published in the United States of America.

I

The sun was setting on the horizon as a lone automobile moved swiftly along the winding roads of the countryside. The driver's destination was a small, abandoned house sitting at the end of a long, gravel driveway. This driver was Phillip Martin, husband to Yvonne Martin and father to his sole child David. The deserted home to which the family traveled was to become their new abode. They had just moved from the city and were now ready to inhabit this humble house. The Martin family had recently converted to Catholicism, thus starting a new and better life. With this change in their spiritual lives, they decided to begin anew also in their physical lifestyles, and so, they moved. As the sun only just left sight, the Martins reached their new home and carried inside the remaining luggage from their old house. Once settled, all were asleep in bed.

The following morning, the first of the family to rise was David. Being a boy of twelve years of age, he had an insatiable desire to explore. His recent target of observation was his new backyard. Vast and thick woodlands began just a few yards from his house and stretched seemingly endlessly over the horizon. Such sights are the usual point of interest in a child's eyes, and it was no different for David. Along with this inquisitiveness came his new appreciation of everything as a creation of God. Since his family converted to Catholicism, David enjoyed life so much more. Now, the world had more purpose. He hastily consumed the breakfast of scrambled eggs and toast prepared for him by his mother; so quickly, that he barely tasted a thing. The boy then dressed appropriately for his journey into the forest. He wore long pants, high socks, and boots, despite the fact that it was summertime. The purpose of this was to protect his skin from contacting poison ivy, to which he was highly allergic. David announced his departure to his mother, gave her a kiss, and bolted for the tree line.

The moment he entered the woodland, the boy's curiosity flourished. Wandering about aimlessly, he observed all there was to see. Little escaped his gaze. David thought to himself how marvelous it was that God created so much and with such flawless detail. As he pondered upon this, he suddenly noticed something in the corner of his eye. He turned and was very much surprised to see a small crucifix hanging from a tree.

"That's strange," he thought. "What's this doing all the way out here?"

David recently learned about crucifixes. He had seen them many times, but only of late discovered their significance and now had great respect for the cross. Pulling the sacred artifact from its place, he inspected it for a name. Engraved along the back of the crucifix was the word "frater." David had no experience with foreign languages, and so dismissed the inscription as unimportant. However, he did not conclude his observation of the small cross. Its design was fantastic, possibly even unique. A very skilled carpenter or wood carver must have fashioned it from the most beautifully perfect piece of wood. The body of the crucified Christ was a flawless imitation of a human being. The cross itself was carved to look like grape vines winding with utter symmetry. Wooden bundles of grapes hung from the crucifix just beneath Our Lord's hands and feet. David was greatly impressed by the care with which the small cross was made. He stared in admiration for a while, returned the crucifix to its place, and then knelt to say a prayer. The boy prayed silently, mouthing the words, which flowed from his heart and soared into heaven. When David finished, he made the Sign of the Cross and rose to his feet. As soon as he did this, a sounded erupted throughout the forest. It was… music? Someone was playing a flute, and what a mournful tune it was! Simply listening to it caused David to feel sad at heart. He felt uneasy at the sound. Something seemed ominous about it, yet the song was so innocently sorrowful that David doubted it was for ill purpose. Regardless, the boy was worried. Who was this strange flutist? Why should he play so sad of a song, and why in the woods? It was all quite odd. Soon, it became too strange for the boy to remain, and he returned home.

David described the occurrence to his parents that night, in the hope that they might be able to explain something.

"I don't know, sweetie," replied Mrs. Martin.

Mr. Martin said nothing, but walked to the back door and opened it. To the surprise of the family, the sad song was still ringing through the forest, setting a somewhat unpleasant air about the night. Yvonne pressed David close to her and looked at her husband with a bewildered countenance.

"I feel..." she said suddenly, "depressed. This music makes me worry for some reason."

Phillip promptly closed the door. "Well," he declared, "perhaps it'll stop before too late. I don't want to hear that all night."

The family then commenced their nightly rosary, and for the entire duration of their prayers, the mysterious flutist played ceaselessly. It was very distracting to David. From time to time, he would stare out the back window, expecting a strange, flute-playing character to emerge from the trees. Much to his relief, one never did. Once finished with the rosary, David prepared himself for bed and went to his room. For a long while, he lay awake, unable to sleep and unable to move his mind from the sorrowful tune which still played outside. Nearly an hour passed before the boy was finally able to rest.

David awoke with a jolt the next morning. His mother had opened a window, thus allowing the endless mourning of the flute to flood into the house. She then closed it quickly. The boy staggered out into the kitchen where his mother stood frozen at the window. Yvonne turned her head slowly toward him.

"I'm sorry, honey," she whispered apologetically, "I didn't think it would still be going on. I'll just turn on the air conditioning."

David sleepily nodded his head and lurched to the dining room where he sat down at the table. The boy remained in his place for a long while, attempting to will the sleep away. All the while, he pondered on the flutist, guessing what his motives might be; that is, if he even had one.

David thought to himself, "What kind of person plays the same song throughout the entire night? It's insane! What could he possibly be doing?"

A theory then dawned on David. Perhaps this mysterious flutist was calling someone… or trying to get somebody's attention at least. He came upon the idea so suddenly, that he jumped from his seat and ran into his room. He then changed for another journey into the forest. Acting almost as a drone, he hastily rushed passed his mother, forgetting breakfast entirely, and ran out the back door, straight into the woods. So fast were his actions that Yvonne had hardly anytime to react, and she merely watched as her son sped off into the unknown. It took a few moments for her to realize what just happened, but she then proceeded to follow David out into the forest. The sad song of the flute blared as it had been for nearly twenty-four hours, and grew louder with every step Mrs. Martin took into the woodland. The boy was no longer in sight, but still she pursued. She ran for about five minutes, but halted when she came upon David kneeling at the masterfully carved crucifix. Yvonne was both surprised and edified by her son's strange actions, so she waited until he finished praying to speak to him.

David stood up a minute later and turned toward his mother.

"David," she said, "if you are going to go outside, I would appreciate it if you would tell me."

"Sorry, Mom," was the reply.

"You can stay out for a little while longer," his mother explained, "but not too long. That flute player worries me."

"Okay," David said.

Yvonne then returned to the house. David waited until she was out of sight to begin his search for the flutist. He followed the mournful music as best he could, attempting to hone in on its loudest point. After searching for about ten minutes, he came upon an area in which the sound was almost deafening; so much so, that the boy had to plug his ears to stand it. He looked about in a nervous panic to see if any person was in view, but saw no one. The only thing to be seen was a fallen tree, which was resting upon the stump of a now non-existent tree. This troubled David greatly, for he now believed the music to be of unworldly origin. It had no physical point of emanation! This seemingly apparent truth became too much for him, and he hurriedly ran back to his home. There he remained for the rest of the day, trying to make sense of what he witnessed. Though, nothing substantial came from his reasoning. The boy was utterly baffled.

II

That night, David sat awake in his bed long after both of his parents were asleep. He could not sleep. The incident boiled in his mind, and he could think of nothing else. After hours of thinking of the subject, David began doubting his ability to see correctly, and finally decided that he required another look.

He put his pants and boots on, grabbed a flashlight and his watch, climbed out his bedroom window, and cautiously ventured into the woods. As he walked deeper into the forest, the somber music grew louder. David, once again, followed the direction in which the sound was most intense. Only this time, he noticed something different about the woodland. The closer he drew to the epicenter of the music, the thicker the trees and foliage seemed to be. This he had not realized before, but did not think it to be of any significance now. After a short while, the boy came upon the fallen tree as before. Much to his surprise, a figure now sat upon the tree, playing a flute beautifully carved from wood. To David, the figure looked like what seemed to be a small child strangely clad in what appeared to be rags or sackcloth, though they covered the entirety of the child's body, and upon his head, he wore a small knit cap. The flutist seemed to be no larger than the size of an infant, yet he sat upright and perfectly balanced on the fallen tree. How could a baby possibly do that? If this was an infant, then why would he be all the way out here, and how could he even know how to play a flute? David slowly walked around the fallen tree in the attempt to see the child's face. As he approached, he shined his flashlight toward the flutist realized that... he had no face, or flesh for that matter. The place where a human face would normally be was replaced by pure darkness. There was nothing there, though David could not see through the child's head. This frightened David to the extent that he let out a short scream. When he did this, the forest child turned towards David, but continued to play the sorrowful tune. David now saw that the child had eyes, though they seemed to merely be glowing orbs floating in his silhouette of a head. The child stared at little Mr. Martin to no end with his illuminated eyes, and yet made no effort to move from his spot. David wanted to run, but something caused him to stay, almost as if his conscience told him to do so. He warily moved toward the mysterious flutist until he stood just paces before him.

"Uh... Hello," yelled David, attempting to speak over the sound, "how are you?"

To this, the forest child did nothing, but kept playing his sad song. David stood silently for a few moments and then said, "My name is David Martin."

Suddenly, the child ceased his flute playing and moved the instrument from his non-existent mouth. He then turned his entire body to face David and stared quietly at him. David was somewhat startled by this. He had not expected that to work, and now he knew not what to say. Both looked at one another in utter silence for a long while, as if they were trying to read each other's mind. Finally, David spoke.

"Who are you?" he asked.

A moment of quiet reigned throughout the woods; that is, until a voice rang out. The voice of a small boy spoke, though not as a child would speak. It spoke more clearly than even the foremost speechmaker. David also noticed that it did not come from the child on the log, but sounded throughout the forest as if it were everywhere.

The voice said, "I am but one of a countless multitude who mourn for that which was lost to us."

David looked about, trying to pinpoint the location of the voice, but it was no use. The voice was in the air. He then looked back at the forest child in understandable confusion.

"Is that you talking?" he inquired.

The small flutist nodded his head slowly, but said nothing. David thought for a moment, hoping to think of a possible question to ask.

"What..." he stuttered, "What did you lose?"

Again, a short silence reigned, and then the child spoke.

"The love of our forebears," he replied.

David was completely bewildered as to the meaning of this, and so, attempted to change the subject.

"Why do you play that sad song all the time?" he asked.

"Sorrow is all that we know," said the infant, "The song is the anguish within our souls, only that which we can feel."

"So, you play it, because you're sad?" David queried.

The forest child nodded his head gravely. "Yes," said he, "for that which we have lost."

David stood, staring into the flutist's non-blinking eyes, and thought of his next question.

He said, "What… I hope you aren't offended by this, but… What are you, exactly? You don't look human."

A long pause reigned, and for a time, the child did nothing. Then, he moved his gaze to some unknown object and spoke.

"We are human," he explained, "That much we can reveal to thee."

David was obviously confused. He tried to ask another question, but was cut off before he got the chance.

"The hour grows late, David Martin. You require rest," said the forest child.

David checked his watch. The flutist was right. It was already three o'clock in the morning. Young Mr. Martin couldn't believe it. Scarcely had an hour gone by in his eyes, yet much longer a time had passed. He started to run back, but then stopped and turned toward the infant.

"Will I see you again?" he asked, "I have so many questions."

The forest child nodded slowly and replied, "We shall remain in this spot for the duration of necessity. Come only at night, for that is the time of darkness and thus secrecy."

As soon as he said this, he once again started playing the depressing tune with his wooden flute. David watched the forest child for a few moments longer, and then returned to his bedroom through the window. Despite feeling wide awake from the night's events, he soon fell asleep from exhaustion.

III

Later that morning, Yvonne woke David from sleep.

"David," she said sweetly, "it's almost ten thirty. Time to get up."

The boy rubbed his eyes, yawned rather loudly, and then stumbled as he tried to stand from his bed. His mother watched him with a confused countenance as he clumsily inched his way to the table and sat down. Her perplexity then turned to concern.

"How could you be so tired?" she asked, "You've been asleep for nearly thirteen hours!"

David made no detectable sign of emotion or movement in reply, but merely let out a short groan. Mrs. Martin suddenly began checking the boy's forehead for a fever but was relieved when she was unsuccessful at finding one. She then sat next to him and stared at his sleepily crinkled face.

"Well," thought Yvonne, "perhaps he just becoming a teenager."

She then exited the room to prepare David's breakfast. It was only minutes before she re-entered with freshly sliced melon, buttered toast, and a glass of orange juice. She placed the meal in front of David and left the room. The boy said his grace to himself and then slowly nibbled away at the toast. Regardless of his outward appearance, David's mind was erupting with the memories of the previous night, and he pondered on the forest child's words.

"'Mourning that which we have lost… The love of our forebears.' To what could he possibly be referring?" David thought, "Did he somehow anger his great-great-grandparents? Who is 'we'?"

He already had plans to return to the fallen tree that night, and he would, hopefully, discover the answers to his questions. The anticipation of his next meeting with the mysterious infant caused him to be nervously anxious, and he remained so throughout the entirety of the day and evening. Much to the surprise of his parents, he made no effort to go outside. He merely sat bright-eyed on his bed, staring out into the forest with the window open, thus allowing the sorrowful tune to fill the house. This came as a slight disturbance to

Yvonne, for the music made her feel somewhat depressed and even guilty. She did not like it whatsoever. The song reminded her of something she could not remember, or had chosen to forget in the past, but she could not place it. Finally, the mournful song absorbed her emotions completely, and she broke down in tears for seemingly no reason at all. Mr. Martin lifted his wife to her feet and inquired as to what the problem might be. Yvonne spoke, but uttered nothing intelligible. Phillip was utterly lost and could think of no means by which to console her. He then turned his attention to the music, which upon hearing, he too felt guilt within his soul.

"David!" he called, "Please close the window!"

The boy obeyed and promptly shut it. Both Mr. and Mrs. Martin breathed a sigh of relief, but still felt the remains of anguish within their hearts for reasons neither of them could explain. David stood watching his parents, bewildered at what he beheld in front of him.

"What happened?" he asked.

His father replied very solemnly, "I... I don't know, son. That music just... makes us feel sad."

Upon saying this, Phillip escorted his wife into the next room, and they both sat down. David felt responsible for their pain, though he could not explain why. A sudden cloud of sadness came over him, and he returned to his room to again look out into the woods.

The nighttime could not come soon enough for David. He had been waiting for it the entire day. Finally, his mother came into his room to announce that it was time to sleep. The boy excitedly prepared for bed and was soon lying down seemingly sound asleep. There he waited until he was certain that both of his parents had also drifted off into slumber. He then rose and readied himself for his journey into the forest. Once again, he grabbed his flashlight and watch, and then climbed out his bedroom window. Minutes later, David was running through the woodland, quickly approaching the place where he had met the forest child. The saddening tune was playing as always and was as loud as ever.

As the boy arrived at the spot of the fallen tree, the music stopped, and the little flutist turned his head toward David.

"Greetings, David Martin," said he, "We are pleased that you have returned."

"Well," replied young Mr. Martin, "I have a lot of questions for you."

The infant nodded slowly, "We shall answer them to the fullest of our capability."

David was about to ask a question he was saving from the previous night, but then remembered the incident with his parents when they heard the music.

He explained, "Today, I had my window open and I was listening to your song. Suddenly, my mom started crying, and my dad..."

He paused, for the forest child seemed to be... crying! The little flutist made no noise or movements, but tears... glowing tears flowed from his "eyes." David could not believe it, nor did he understand.

"What's wrong?" he queried, "Why are you crying?"

The child shook his head. "It matters not," he stated, "not now."

David was understandably confused but continued with the question.

"Why does your music bother my parents, but not me?" he asked.

"The answer to this," the infant said gravely, "shall be answered at the adequate time. You must wait."

As he said this, the tears ceased to emanate from his face.

David stared at the mysterious child for a few moments, hoping to somehow discover his secrets, but then resumed his inquiries.

"How is it that you can play a flute?" he asked, "I mean, you're just a baby, right?"

The little flutist sat quietly upon his perch, saying nothing for a short while. Then, he spoke, "We are human, though we are no longer bound to the inabilities of this world. The infant being you see before you is merely a form. That in which we were last seen by mankind."

It suddenly dawned on David. "You're... dead?" he yelled.

The forest child bowed his head and nodded solemnly. Young Mr. Martin felt a great sense of fear within his heart. He wanted to run, but again, his conscience made him stay.

"So," he started, "you're like a ghost."

"Not entirely," was the reply, "but you may call us what you wish."

David felt a bit unsteady. "Okay," he said abruptly.

He now began to understand as to why the child looked the way he did, but the absence of his face made no sense.

He asked, "What happened to your face? If you're a human, then why don't you have one?"

"No man saw our face as we were alive; therefore, we have not one to show man now," explained the flutist.

David thought for a moment and then posed the question, "I hope you don't mind me asking, but how did you die?"

"By the will of our forebears," declared the child in a quieted voice. He then began to cry once more.

Young Mr. Martin attempted to piece together what he had heard so far. "So, you lost the love of your forebears," stated David, "and they killed you?"

"We never achieved their love, David Martin. By their selfishness, we were murdered. By it, we were removed from their lives."

"But why?" demanded David, "Why did they kill you? You were just a baby!" He stopped for a moment to collect his thoughts. "What kind of person would murder a baby?"

The forest child turned his head and looked away from David.

Young Mr. Martin then asked, "Why would your grandparents kill you?"

The infant returned his gaze to David. "Not our grandparents, David Martin," he explained, "but our own parents. It is by their will that we were murdered."

David was now upset. "What is this 'we' stuff?" he asked, "Who is 'we'?"

The little flutist sat in silence, staring blankly at young Mr. Martin. Suddenly, a large breeze blew throughout the forest. It was so forceful, that it ripped leaves from the trees, carried them in a large mass, and then blasted toward David. He braced himself and covered his face as the leaves rushed passed him. When he opened his eyes, there stood about him an innumerable army of forest children, holding the exact appearance of the one resting on the fallen tree. David cringed in fear at the sight of them. They were so many, more than he could ever count. They surrounded him in a solid formation that could be broken by no earthly force. David was trapped! He looked at them all with a countenance of pure fright, and they all gazed back at him with seemingly blank and lost faces. Silence reigned throughout the entire woodland. Nothing moved. David then wondered if this multitude of multitudes might be waiting for him to say something. He erected his posture of his fullest height, mustered up all the courage within his soul, and spoke.

"Who are you?" he demanded.

The endless sea of faceless infants sounded the reply with one voice, which shook the earth and rattled the trees. "We are they who lost the love of their forebears. We are they who lost our lives at the hands of selfishness. We are they who were murdered by those who bore us."

David was utterly humbled by the dominance displayed by the forest children, yet he continued. He asked, "And you mourn because they killed you? You're sad, because you didn't get the chance to live?"

As David said this, another breeze came through, and as it blew passed, the countless multitude disintegrated as dust in the wind. All was then quiet.

"Nay," said a voice abruptly.

David turned to the little flutist sitting upon the fallen tree.

The infant continued, "We mourn, David Martin, for our forebears, not for ourselves. We mourn for their souls, for as they destroyed our lives, they have also destroyed their own souls. That is the reason for which we mourn. With the loss of the love of those who bore us came, too, the loss of the chance to see them in a loving manner."

David was puzzled.

"But," he started, "where did all of those other forest babies go?"

"To their final resting place," replied the little flutist, "It is the realm of natural happiness made by Almighty God for those who never willingly committed evil, but never received the waters of Baptism. It is the last destination of all who lost their lives before coming into this world, whether by murder or natural death. To humanity, it has come to be known as 'Limbo'."

It then dawned on David that this was all connected to Catholicism, the religion to which his family had recently converted.

"You mean… these babies' parents will go to Hell?" he asked, "All of them?"

Tears once again flowed from the forest child's eyes "If they do not repent for the evil they have wrought, then... Yes, they shall perish," he answered. The infant then covered his face with his hands.

David was suddenly overcome by a deep sense of sorrow, and he fell to his knees with his head hanging in utter sadness. "I can't believe it," he whispered, "All of those people…" He looked up at the forest child. "How come nobody stops them from killing their children? Isn't it illegal?"

The infant turned his gaze to David with a start. "Do you not know?" he asked.

"Know what?" replied young Mr. Martin.

The little flutist hung his head and shook it sadly. He then dissipated into the night without saying another word.

"Wait!" yelled David, "What do I need to know?"

The child's voice spoke, "We shall reveal it to thee when you return, if, at that time, you still do not know."

David then asked, "Can I tell any of this to my parents?"

It was silent for a long while. David even contemplated leaving in the thought that the infant had left. However, then the child spoke one last time for the night.

"If you find it necessary to do so," was the reply.

David then checked his watch. "Three o'clock in the morning. That's strange," thought the boy. "It's the same time as last night."

He brushed this off as merely a coincidence and rushed back to his bedroom window, which upon entering, he heard the sad music of the flute recommence. He then closed his window and was soon asleep.

IV

David awoke to the sound of his mother calling him from sleep.

"David," she whispered with a uniquely motherly tenderness, "it's time to get up, sweetheart."

The boy sat up slowly and rubbed his eyes, which were so squinted that they seemed completely shut. He then stood at the side of his bed, but failed to move forward. Yvonne did not bother to watch him as she did before. She assumed that his unnaturally late risings were merely a new trend accompanying his increase in age. As soon as his mother left the room, David sat back down on his bed. Not only was he exhausted, but also somewhat melancholic. He felt a festering perplexity within his heart that translated into utter sadness. The concluding conversation of the previous night had a great impact on him. What could it possibly be that he didn't know, or that he needed to know? What if it was serious? That fact of his ignorance bothered him to such a degree that he felt he might even cry. He was bitterly lost.

Suddenly, he remembered the last bit of the conversation. The forest child granted him permission to tell his parents of the recent events in the woods. Excited, David jumped from his bed and sped into the living room where Yvonne was mopping the floor.

"Mom," he stated anxiously, "I need to tell you something."

"Sure, honey. What is it?" she replied sweetly.

David was about to speak, but then realized that the news of his venturing into the woods at night, especially while the sad flute music was still playing, would not be very pleasing to his mother. He held his breath for a moment, trying to think of an appropriate way to organize his words. The boy then mustered up his courage and spoke.

"Okay," he explained, "so, for the past two nights, I have sneaked out into the woods and..."

"David!" Yvonne interrupted, "Why in the world would you do that? Don't you know it's dangerous?"

"Mom," David replied calmly, "I'm sorry, but... could I finish?"

His mother wanted to say something, but merely nodded her head as she put her hands firmly on her hips.

"All right," he continued, "I went into the woods, because I really wanted to find out who the flutist was. The other day, when you came after me into the forest, I was looking for him, but I knelt down to pray that I would find him. Then you came, but after you went home, I followed the music. I walked really far until the music sounded close, but when I looked at the place where it was coming from, nobody was there. So, I came home. Later that night, something told me to go check again. So, I waited until you and Dad were asleep, and then I climbed out my window and went looking again. This time, I found him."

By this time, Yvonne was slightly captivated by the story, and so, began to ask questions.

"What did he look like?" she inquired.

"Well, that's the weird part," declared David.

"Weird?"

"Yeah. He is the same size as a baby, and he looks human, but he… has no face."

This gave his mother a deep sense of disbelief.

"No face? David, I think you were dreaming," replied Yvonne.

"No, I wasn't!" urged the boy, "He's real! I talked to him. I've been talking to him for the past two nights. That's what I'm trying to tell you! He's a kid, but he's dead. But somehow, he's alive and talking and even without a mouth, he still plays the flute. His face is just nothing, and he has eyes that are like little lights that float in his head. He wears really worn clothes, except… except his hat. He wears a little sleep time hat… like the babies in the nursery at the hospital."

Yvonne merely stared at her son in confusion.

She then spoke, "That must have been some dream you had, sweetheart."

"Mom," claimed David, "I wasn't dreaming! I spent hours talking to him! That's why I'm always so tired in the morning!"

Upon hearing these words, his mother looked toward a window facing the backyard. She then returned her gaze to David.

"All right, David," she stated, "Maybe you did go out into the woods these past few nights, but, honey, it's just not possible for something like that to happen. Dead people don't just come back to life and start talking to people."

"Well," retorted the boy, "he did talk to me. But it did take a while to get him to talk. He didn't even look at me until I said my name."

"You told your name to a stranger?" Yvonne exclaimed, "David! Do you not listen to anything I teach you?"

"But it got him to talk to me," he told her, "and I don't really see him as a stranger. He's really nice. I don't know. I feel safe with him."

His mother was now upset and bewildered. Who was this person? Why would he trick someone into thinking he was dead? Yvonne could not understand it. She wanted to know more, yet was afraid to ask. A thousand worries plagued her as she pondered on the subject. Taking a deep breath, she spoke.

"David, tell me what you talked about with this… person," she demanded.

David thought for a moment, attempting to recall precisely what had been said. "After I finally got him to pay attention to me, I asked him who he was. He said something like, 'We are they who lost… the love of something.' I don't remember exactly. I asked him why he was playing the flute, and he said that it was because he… or they were sad. He always said 'we' when he talked about himself. I asked him why last night, and suddenly there were thousands of them… millions even! You should've seen it, Mom. There were so many of them!"

"Of what?" asked Yvonne.

"Well," replied David, "I don't know what they are really. But I have just thought of them as forest children. They are like little babies who live in the woods. But yeah, that's why he says 'we' a lot."

Yvonne was understandably lost. She knew not what to make of the situation. One thing of which she was certain was that David would never go out into those woods again to speak to some stranger.

"David," she commanded, " you are not...."

"Mom," David interjected, "I have to go back tonight. He told me that there is something I don't know, and I feel like I need to know what it is. He was really sad when I didn't know what it was. I have to know."

Yvonne would not be moved, or so she thought. A strange feeling came over her, and she felt the urge to allow David to fulfill his desire. She suddenly felt that his want was somewhat necessary. Mrs. Martin arched her brow as her heart sank. This seemed so counter-intuitive, yet vital.

"All right," she stated reluctantly.

David was mutually shocked at his mother's words. He froze for a short while, but then thanked her as he gave her a hug and walked into his room.

For the remainder of the day, the Martin household was silent. Even when Mr. Martin returned home from work, hardly a word was said, much to his surprise. Occasionally, Phillip attempted to discover what the problem was, but was every time denied an answer.

The sun set that evening with a strange quietness. It was unsettling, even slightly ominous. The moon and the stars soon appeared across the night sky. David waited until the usual time and opened his window. Suddenly, he felt a hand touch his shoulder. Yvonne turned her son around and spoke to him.

"David," she asked, "are you sure you want to do this?"

"No, Mom," he replied, "I need to do this."

David then climbed out his window and walked into the forest. Yvonne stood watching him until she could see him no more. Then, she began to follow him. The sorrowful music played as it nearly always did.

The boy walked along the trail he knew led to the forest child. Soon, he came upon the thickening trees as he did the two previous nights. David ventured a few steps further and was pleased to find the forest child playing his flute.

"Hello," he declared as he took his place before the mysterious flutist.

The infant ceased playing his instrument and faced David.

"Greetings, David Martin," replied the flutist, "It gladdens us to see you again."

Yvonne stopped in her tracks. It was the first time in three days that she had not heard the music playing, and now that it was gone, she felt oddly unsteady. Something had to be very wrong.

She called out, "David!"

No answer returned. It was, as she had feared. The flute player had stolen her David! Yvonne ran aimlessly, calling to David, but no response ever came. The apparent reality became too much for her, and she fainted mid-stride. She awoke moments later in tears. Why did she let him come outside again? Suddenly, a dominant, yet calming voice spoke.

"Yvonne, fear not," it explained, "David is alive, safe, and well. He hears you not. Return home and rest."

Mrs. Martin was both bewildered and frightened. A strange voice from nowhere was calling her by name and telling her to go home. Why would she listen to it? She glanced here and there about her surroundings, but saw no one. All of a sudden, someone grabbed her arm. She shrieked and slapped the person. Then, she realized that it was her husband.

"Sweetheart, what are you doing out here at this time of night? Come back to the house," demanded Phillip.

Yvonne wanted to continue searching for David, but something told her that the mysterious voice was trustworthy, and she returned home with Mr. Martin.

"So," stated David, "I still don't know what you were talking about last night. Could you tell me?"

The forest child expressed a sound, which resembled a sorrowful sigh.

"We had hoped that we would not be your informant," explained the infant, "but it is of great importance that you know this. As you recall from the previous night, we revealed to you how our deaths came to be."

"Yes," replied young Mr. Martin, "Your parents killed you."

The forest child paused.

"Not entirely," said he, "It was by their will, by their desire, and by their selfishness that we were delivered into the hands of murderers."

David inquired, "Well, then how is it possible that all of those babies from last night were killed without anyone noticing? You'd think someone would stop it."

The infant continued, "There are those who attempt to save us, but we all are not so lucky as to be saved before it is too late. David Martin, this evil in which the innocent are slain is known, in this world, as 'abortion'. It is the epitome of human greed. Mankind has lost its respect for the sacredness of life. This massacre has been a legalized service for many selfish persons for far too long."

"Wait!" exclaimed the boy, "You mean that this is legal? They can kill babies without going to jail?"

The little flutist nodded his head gravely.

"'Tis the disturbing reality of this world," he stated in a bitter sadness.

David could not believe it. He was in shock. All of these innocent babies were being slaughtered as mere inconveniences and with no one there to save them. The fact of its existence was horrifying to realize.

"All of those babies..." whispered young Mr. Martin, "They're all... dead? They're dead because of this?"

The infant again nodded as tears began streaming from his eyes. David's eyes, too, filled with tears. The thought of babies being slaughtered was terrible enough, but for them to be slaughtered by the will of their very own parents was something else entirely. He was grateful that his parents did not take part in such an atrocity. David looked up at the flutist.

"So," he said, attempting to regain his composure, "this is what happened to you, too?"

The forest child nodded once more.

"Do you hate your parents for it?" David asked.

"Never. My love shall always be with them," replied the infant, "whether or not they choose to accept it."

David noticed that this was the first time that he had heard the infant speak only of himself. He took the opportunity to ask a specific question.

"What were their names?" the boy inquired.

The little flutist said nothing, but merely sat on his perch, staring at David. Silence reigned for a long while as the two children gazed at one another in thought. Then, without saying a word, the infant removed a large piece of bark from the fallen tree and began carving something into it with his flute. He soon finished his scratching, dropped the fragment to the ground, and dissipated into the night. David slowly approached the piece of bark and attempted to read it. It showed the word, "frater."

"Hey!" thought young Mr. Martin, "That's the same word that was on the crucifix hanging on the tree! But what does it mean?"

David rushed to the spot where the cross hung and knelt down. There he closed his eyes in prayer.

V

David opened his eyes, and was confused to see sunlight shining through the forest. He had fallen asleep, yet still remained in his kneeling position. He had not moved an inch! It was indeed fascinating, but he wasted no time with it. He rushed home to ask his parents the meaning of the inscription on the bark. So excited and anxious was David that he nearly leapt through his open window and onto his bed. He sped into the kitchen where both of his parents sat, eating an early morning breakfast.

"David!" yelled Yvonne as she stood and gave him a loving embrace.

Phillip was utterly lost.

"Uh… Good morning, son," he stated confusedly, "What are you doing up so early?"

"Dad," David stated firmly, "I have something really important to talk about."

Both Mr. and Mrs. Martin were surprised at the determination with which the boy spoke. They turned their full and undivided attention to him.

"All right," he stated, "What does this mean?"

He then placed the piece of bark on the table. Phillip and Yvonne studied the word and looked at one another.

"Well," explained Phillip, "it's Latin. I think it means 'father,' right?"

"No," replied Mrs. Martin, "that is 'pater.' I think 'frater' means 'brother.' David, where did you get this?"

"The forest child gave it to me," he announced triumphantly.

"Forest child?" asked Mr. Martin.

"Yes," explained Yvonne, "that is what David calls the flutist."

"You saw him?" inquired Phillip, "What did he look like?"

"Uh, it's complicated," answered Yvonne.

She then turned back to David and spoke, "Did you find out who he is?"

"Well," David started, "I don't know if you know about this, but there is a really bad thing happening where parents have their babies killed. The flutist is one of them, but he's like a ghost. He came back, even after being murdered. It's called 'abortion'."

He stopped. Both of his parents were crying.

"Mom? Dad?" he uttered somewhat lost, "What's the matter?"

He received no answer, for they sobbed uncontrollably. Neither of them could speak.

"Can you please tell me what's going on?" he yelled in a frightened voice, "You're scaring me!"

Phillip was the first to regain a fraction of his composure.

"I'm sorry, son," he coughed, "You must understand…"

"Understand what?" demanded David.

"Before you were born," Mr. Martin explained, "we were very different people. We didn't have our morals entirely straight. We did some very bad things."

"What do you mean?" whispered the boy.

"David," cried Yvonne, "please forgive us, sweetheart. We can never forgive ourselves for what we did."

"What?" David exclaimed in bitter perplexity.

"Son," Phillip declared with tears flowing down his face, "you would have had… a brother, but –"

"But what?" David stopped. It all came together. He now understood.

"What?" he yelled on the verge of tears. "No! Not you, too!"

He collapsed to the floor and cried repeatedly, "No! It can't be! How?"

Yvonne attempted to calm him by taking hold of his hand, but David batted her hand away and ran into his room.

"No, David!" exclaimed distraught Mrs. Martin as she chased after him.

Phillip watched as she disappeared into David's room. Suddenly, he heard her yell, "Come back, honey!"

Mr. Martin rushed into the room to find his wife sobbing on the bed, the window flung open, and David running away in the distance. Everything was falling apart. All hope seemed lost.

David ran blinded by his tears through the forest. He had no intended destination. He only wanted to get as far away from his parents as possible. They had his brother murdered! He could scarcely believe it. His whole world was shattering. Catching a protruding root with his foot, David tripped and fell to the ground. With his face now in the dirt, he wept at the loss of his brother and the selfishness of his parents. How could they? How could they have known, yet still have agreed to it? How could this be? David could hardly think.

He lifted his head to see where he was. Standing but a few paces before him was the forest child. David jumped to his feet and immediately embraced the little flutist.

"So," declared the infant, "I see that you now know."

David was so choked with sorrow that he struggled to speak. He merely remained hugging the child, who was his brother. The little one took a step back and pressed his tiny hand to David's face.

"What will you do now?" asked young Mr. Martin.

The infant whispered, "I shall merely remain in my dwelling place, forever grieving the loss of my parents'... our parents' love."

Tears then began streaming from his eyes as well. He opened his small arms and embraced David. The two brothers hugged one another for a long while, refusing to leave each other. Abruptly, the forest child loosened his grip. David glanced at him in confusion, but then realized that the infant was staring at something. Young Mr. Martin turned around and saw his parents standing about a dozen paces behind him. The sight, which Phillip and Yvonne witnessed before them, frightened them both. Their two sons, living and dead, were in front of them, and both now seemingly despised them. Mr. and Mrs. Martin watched their children with the caring eyes of loving parents. David released the forest child and stood up.

"I think there's something you need to say… to **him**!" yelled David as he pointed at his brother.

Mr. and Mrs. Martin nodded their heads with tears still flowing from their eyes. Both crouched down and stared at the infant with remorseful thoughts.

"Forgive us, sweetheart," whispered Yvonne in a choked voice.

"We're so sorry, son," sobbed Phillip.

The little flutist slowly approached them, but halted just a step before them. He looked into their eyes as they gazed sorrowfully back into his. The child then lifted his hands and extended them toward his parents. Phillip and Yvonne lightly grabbed them and, once again, began sobbing upon doing so. With his tiny fingers, the forest child caressed his parents' hands. He then loosed his hold of them and rejoined David.

"Their love is sincere," declared the infant as he began to cry.

"We have confessed our sins," explained Mrs. Martin, "and have vowed to do penance for the rest of our lives."

The child sounded a sigh. As he did this, a strong gust developed and blew all around the Martins. So strong was the wind, that all had to shield their eyes. When the blast subsided, everyone looked at the little flutist. His face was glowing. The light it radiated was almost blinding. Suddenly, it pulsed, emitting a burst of light, which did blind all for a moment. When they opened their eyes, there standing before them was a boy of fifteen years of age, clothed in sackcloth. Yvonne gasped and started to cry more.

"He's so handsome…" she stated in bitter sadness as she dug her face into Phillip's shoulder.

The boy then spoke, "Almighty God has granted you this blessing that you may go about this world, preaching the evils of abortion. In His boundless mercy, He has granted you the blessing of this moment as a memory."

David now looked up at his brother. He could hardly believe his eyes. "You're my brother," he whispered with a distraught smile.

The forest child looked down at David. "Yes, I am," he replied as he rubbed his younger brother's head, "but I fear that I must go now. My time here is spent."

"No!" urged David, as tears formed in his eyes, "There's so much I want to talk about with you."

"We may, one day, have time for that," explained the boy, "as long as you remain in the friendship of God and submit your entire life to His most Holy Will. Do you understand?"

"Yes," confirmed young Mr. Martin.

The forest child then turned toward his parents and smiled. "I thank you, Mother and Father," he declared. "I am gladdened to know that you have changed your ways and have repented. Your love for me is now as mine has always been for you. But now I must bid you 'farewell'."

"But," started Phillip, "will we ever see you again, son?"

The forest child cast a thoughtful look to his parents.

"Perhaps, you shall," he explained. "It is only by the permission of Our Lord that we might, once again, see one another. That is for you to beg of Him. Achieve everlasting happiness, and perhaps Almighty God shall grant you and me the blessing of reunion. However, I cannot enter into the kingdom of Heaven, for I never received the waters of Baptism. My place is in the realm of natural happiness. There it shall be, if God wills it to be so, that you and I shall certainly again meet."

He then turned and began to walk away.

"Wait!" yelled David suddenly.

The flutist halted his pace and drew his attention to his brother. David grabbed his hand, as if to make the boy stay, and then looked at his parents.

"What would you have named him?" he posed.

Phillip and Yvonne looked at one another, and, by the grace of God, they knew exactly what name they would give him. They stared back at their two sons and spoke with one voice. "Patrick," they announced.

Patrick nodded to them in thanks and turned his gaze toward David.

"Well, Pat," stated David as he began to cry, "It looks like I won't be seeing you for a long time."

The boy smiled with tears in his eyes.

"I shall be happily waiting for you, my brother," he declared.

The two brothers embraced one another for the last time and then separated. David joined his parents, and the three watched as Patrick smiled at them and waved. As they returned the gesture, the young flutist suddenly glowed with a great light. So bright was it, that they could not distinguish his features. Then suddenly, the light burst into nothingness, and the vision of the boy was no more.

Phillip looked up into sky and whispered, "Be at peace, Patrick."

The Martin family then returned home and prayed in thanksgiving. They thanked God for His unforgettable blessing and prayed for the grace to grant that they all would see Patrick once again.

THE END

Now that you have taken the time to read this tale, please take one more minute of your time to say a prayer for the little ones of innocence who have lost their lives at the whims of those who bore them.

May God bless you.

ISBN-13: 978-1492931522

The Lost Children. Kevin D.N. Lawson. Copyright © September 22, 2012. All Rights Reserved.

Published in the United States of America.

Made in the USA
Lexington, KY
03 March 2017